The Manners Heist

By Yolanda Villafana

Illustrated by Deborah Delaney

For those who teach.

This book is dedicated to our good friend, Miss Donna, who we lost too soon. She brought joy and laughter into every life she touched. She was a beloved teacher and friend.

The LORD was full of praise. "Well done, good and faithful servant."
Matthew 25:21

One tragic day in Miss Donna's classroom...

Miss Donna

a robber snuck in
and stole the
manners away.

No please,
no thank you
was heard that day.

No listening,
no obeying,
not a kind word to say!

Children running and screaming.
No learning in sight.

The room was in shambles.
Poor Miss Donna looked a fright!

"There has been a manners heist!"

Miss Donna exclaimed.

Children without manners.

Oh, what a shame!

Miss Donna needed help.

She knew what to do.

She called Detective Rodrigo to search for a clue.

Detective Rodrigo surveyed the scene.

Children whining, demanding, and shouting.

No children with manners in sight.

A crime had been committed.

Miss Donna was right.

He talked to the children one by one.
The same story repeated by everyone.
No please or thank you was used at home.
Demanding and pouting was how it was done.

The children never cleaned their rooms.

Chores were a bore.

When they broke a toy, Mommy just ran to the store.

Detective Rodrigo asked each child a question. *"If you want something, what should you do?"*

"Take it!" They shouted. He shook his head sadly and Miss Donna looked blue.

"Uh-huh! That's it! I've solved the case!"
Detective Rodrigo gathered the children with all posthaste.

Miss Donna was excited to discover who was the thief.
To have the manners returned, what a relief!

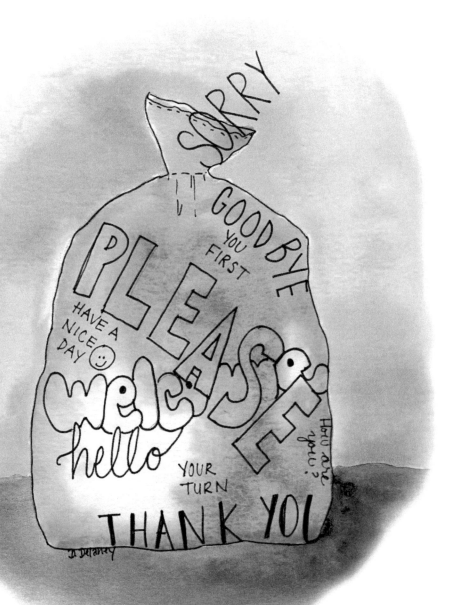

It was an inside job
Detective Rodrigo
concluded.

He took out his notebook
and laid out his findings.

Then he stepped up to the
board and started writing.

"An inside job!" Miss Donna proclaimed. She looked at her class and wondered who was to blame.

The children looked at each other, pointing fingers every which way. Detective Rodrigo said to point them their way.

On the board, Detective Rodrigo wrote one simple rule:

TREAT OTHERS AS YOU WOULD LIKE TO BE **TREATED**

D. Delaney

As the children read that rule, it sank deep in their hearts.

"Treat others as you would like to be treated," they repeated.

If I want kindness, I must be kind.

If I want respect, I must be respectful.

If I want to be heard, I must listen.

If I want a friend, I must be a friend.

"We're sorry, Miss Donna, we stole the manners away. We understand and from now on our please and thank you we'll say."

Miss Donna just smiled that sweet smile of hers. For kindness is a gift and all wrongs it will cure.

Detective Rodrigo picked up his things and started to leave.

Another case solved.

His heart was well pleased.

This manners heist successfully solved.

For as he walked out the door, he heard "thank you" and "please."

Miss Donna was aglow as she looked at her class.

A lesson well learned will be remembered and last.

Her heart full of love for each and everyone.

Her job for that day completed and well done.

Well
DONE
Miss Donna

Made in the USA
San Bernardino, CA
07 May 2018